Cute and Cuddly: Baby Animals

BEAR CUBS

By Grace Elora

Gareth Stevens Publishing

Please visit our Web site, www.garethstevens.com. For a free color catalog of all our high-quality books, call toll free 1-800-542-2595 or fax 1-877-542-2596.

Library of Congress Cataloging-in-Publication Data

Elora, Grace.
Bear cubs / Grace Elora.
p. cm. — (Cute and cuddly—baby animals)
ISBN 978-1-4339-4499-4 (library binding)
ISBN 978-1-4339-4500-7 (pbk.)
ISBN 978-1-4339-4501-4 (6-pack)
1. Bear cubs—Juvenile literature. I. Title.
QL737.C27E475 2011
599.78′139—dc22

2010035610

First Edition

Published in 2011 by
Gareth Stevens Publishing
111 East 14th Street, Suite 349
New York, NY 10003

Editor: Therese Shea
Designer: Andrea Davison-Bartolotta

Photo credits: Cover, pp. 1, 3, 5, 9, 17, 19, 21, 24 (honey) Shutterstock.com; pp. 7, 13, 15, 23, 24 (panda, polar bear) Thinkstock.com; p. 11 China Photos/Getty Images.

Printed in the United States of America

CPSIA compliance information: Batch #CW11GS: For further information contact Gareth Stevens, New York, New York at 1-800-542-2595.

BEAR CUBS

A cub is a baby bear.

Cubs are born
in winter.

Cubs live in holes in the ground. Cubs live in trees.

Cubs have no fur at first. Their eyes are closed.

Polar bear cubs grow white fur.

Panda bear cubs grow black and white fur.

Mother bears keep cubs safe. They stay close for 2 years.

Cubs like to eat. They eat plants.

Cubs eat fish. They like to swim.

Cubs eat honey. They go up trees.

Words to Know

honey

panda

polar bear